FARMER BILL

BRAIN
Fish, walnuts, & flax seeds, dark green leafy vegetables.

EYES
Yellow fruits and vegetables like carrots cantaloupe, sweet potatoes & butternut squash; spinach, eggs.

SKIN
Low fat dairy products, strawberries, blueberries, blackberries. Salmon, turkey, tuna, brazil nuts, green tea. Water & sunscreen.

HEART
Red & purple fruits and veggies like red grapes, cherries, berries, plums. Lean meats, peas, beans, spinach & O.J. Exercise.

IMMUNE SYSTEM
Store bought wild mushrooms (shitake, maitake, and oyster) and garlic. Sleep.

BONES
Low fat dairy products like milk, yogurt & cheese; kale, collard greens. Exercise & sunshine.

INTESTINES
Whole grains, raspberries, pears, yogurt. Water.

-BS

This Is My Book

This book is dedicated to stewards
of the land and sea and tillers of the soil,
past, present and future.

JJ
STEERS
BILLY

Tractor Mac, LLC, Roxbury, CT 06783 USA
Visit www.tractormac.com

Tractor Mac
FARMER'S MARKET
Plow to Plate® Special Edition
Written and Illustrated by Billy Steers

*This book is dedicated to stewards of the land and sea
and tillers of the soil, past, present and future.*

"Someone ate my piece of birthday cake," said Carla the chicken one sunny morning on Stony Meadow Farm. "I was saving it as a treat for when it got nice and stale," she clucked.

"Hmmm," said Tractor Mac.

"Somebody got into the garbage cans," cried Goat Walter.
"And it wasn't me!" he added.

"Ahh," said Tractor Mac.

"Something raided the pantry," meowed Pepper the cat. "They ate all the sugar and lard!"

"I see," said Tractor Mac.

"I think I know who is behind all of this," sighed Tractor Mac. "Let's pay a visit to our friends Pete and Paul."

They found Pete and his brother Paul in their pen.
"Yuck! What is that smell?" said Carla. "Just stuff we
found," replied Pete. "Eating is our favorite hobby,"
grunted Paul happily.

"Eating and snacking," agreed his brother.

Pigs

COOKIES

"Do you even know what you're eating?" asked Tractor Mac.

"Uhh…something brown, I think," answered Paul.

"If you like food, you'll like the Farmer's Market," said the big red tractor.

"Farmer Bill is bringing you with us today. There's loads of freshly made goods and well grown food."

"Better than what you're eating right now," added Carla.

"Food?" asked Pete. "Like at the fair?" asked Paul. "I love fair food! French fries, fried dough, fried onions, …fried anything! Cotton candy, ice cream, salted pretzels, fudge brownies and soda pop!"

"Fair food is GREAT food!" squealed Paul. "Fair food is barely FAIR food, not great food," corrected Tractor Mac.

"He's right, Paul," said Pete. "Remember what happened last year at the fair when you ate all that junk food?"

"Oh yeah," sighed Paul. "I felt awful for a week! I don't ever want to feel that way again!"

When they got to the Farmer's Market it was busy as usual. "Wow!" exclaimed Paul. "All the neighboring farmers and growers are here," said Pete. Booths were filled with fruits, vegetables, nuts and seeds. Tables held milk and cheese, eggs and honey.

Tucker Pickup tooted his horn. "Machines like Tractor Mac and I need fresh gas and new oil regularly to keep us running smoothly."

"You need balance and variety, like the foods found here to keep you healthy and strong," added Tractor Mac.

"Mmm...that's a good smell!" said Pete. "There are many different and healthy ways to prepare food," said Tractor Mac.

"You can grill, bake or broil, sauté or steam."

"I like mine raw!" cheered Paul.

The next day the animals at Stony Meadow Farm were excited.
The day after a Farmer's Market meant good food for all.

"Hey! Someone took my melon," said Carla.

"Somebody got into the vegetables!" cried Goat Walter. "…And it wasn't me!" he added.

"Something raided the pantry again," meowed Pepper the cat.

"But only the bowls are missing."

"We thought we'd put out a 'Locally grown' spread for all of us," laughed Pete. "Snacks and sweets are OK for a treat, but real food is GREAT food!" said Paul.

"Eating fresh and mostly green will
keep you healthy and keep you lean,"
smiled Tractor Mac.

SAUTEED KALE

This is one of our favorite dishes to make!
Serves 2-4 people

One bunch Kale
1-2 Garlic Cloves
Salt and Pepper
Extra Virgin Olive Oil

Place your farm fresh kale in a bowl of water and let dirt settle to the bottom. Lift kale out of the bowl, pat dry and gently tear off of the rib. Rough chop the leaves to equal small bites. Mince 1-2 garlic cloves or slice very thin, set aside. Bring a pot of water to a boil, salt generously when water is boiling. Place kale in boiling water and blanch for 1 minute, remove from water. Heat a sauté pan on medium high heat. Drizzle olive oil in the pan, add garlic, and quick sauté until fragrant. Place kale in pan, and sauté until cooked, season w/salt and pepper. Enjoy!!!

APPLESAUCE

3 Pounds Apples, peeled, quartered
Local Honey (optional)
Fresh Lemon Juice
Cinnamon or Allspice or Cardamom (optional)

Prepare apples and place in pot on stove with water (about 1/4 cup), cover, and cook until apples are tender. Taste and sweeten with honey and lemon juice. Add spices. Simmer for about 5 minutes. Mash a little more with fork and let cool. Enjoy.

CONNECTICUT BLUEBERRY MUFFINS

2-1/2 Cups Unbleached All Purpose Flour
  or Whole Wheat Pastry Flour
  or a combination of both
2 Teaspoons Baking Powder
1 Teaspoon Baking Soda
1/2 Teaspoon Salt
1/2 Cup packed Light Brown Sugar
2 Farm Eggs, lightly beaten
1-1/3 Cups Fresh Milk room temperature
1/2 Cup melted unsalted Butter
1-1/2 Teaspoons Vanilla Extract
1-1/2 Cups Blueberries

Preheat oven to 375°. Butter muffin tin. Mix dry ingredients together. Mix wet ingredients together, meaning the eggs, milk, melted butter, vanilla extract. Toss fresh blueberries w/one teaspoon lemon zest and one tablespoon flour in a separate bowl. Add the wet to the dry, careful not to over mix, just a few swift strokes with a spoon or spatula until blended. Add blueberries to the batter. Scoop into muffin tins, and place in upper third of the oven, and bake until brown and well risen, about 25 minutes.

BASIL PESTO

1 Cup packed Basil
3 Tablespoons roasted Pine Nuts
3 roasted Garlic Cloves
Salt to taste
Olive Oil

Roast pine nuts in a preheated 350° oven for 5-7 minutes or until lightly golden. Place garlic cloves with skins on in a small saucepan, cover cloves with olive oil, and cook on low heat until cloves skin start to color, and inside feels soft. Remove cloves from skin.

Place basil, pine nuts, and garlic in a food processor and pulse to combine (or use a mortar and pestle). Drizzle olive oil from the roasted garlic pan, and process until everything is combined. Taste and add salt if needed.

When finished cover pesto directly with plastic wrap so it does not darken. Enjoy with pasta, pan seared scallops or your favorite vegetable.

Fruits and vegetables come in many different colors and each color has a different job in keeping your body in tip-top shape. Eat a rainbow to be at your healthiest.

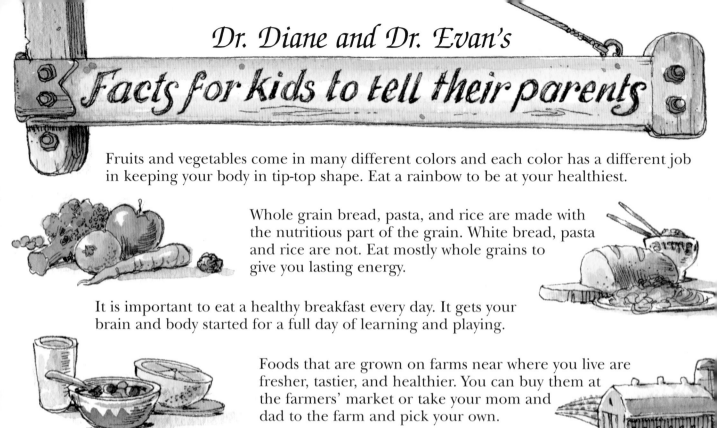

Whole grain bread, pasta, and rice are made with the nutritious part of the grain. White bread, pasta and rice are not. Eat mostly whole grains to give you lasting energy.

It is important to eat a healthy breakfast every day. It gets your brain and body started for a full day of learning and playing.

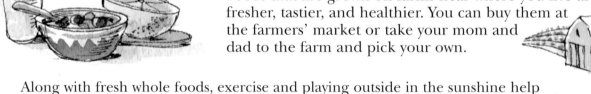

Foods that are grown on farms near where you live are fresher, tastier, and healthier. You can buy them at the farmers' market or take your mom and dad to the farm and pick your own.

Along with fresh whole foods, exercise and playing outside in the sunshine help your heart, muscles and bones grow healthy and strong.